SCARECROWS
OF NECUM TEUCH

THE SCARECROWS OF NECUM TEUCH

ANGELLA GEDDES

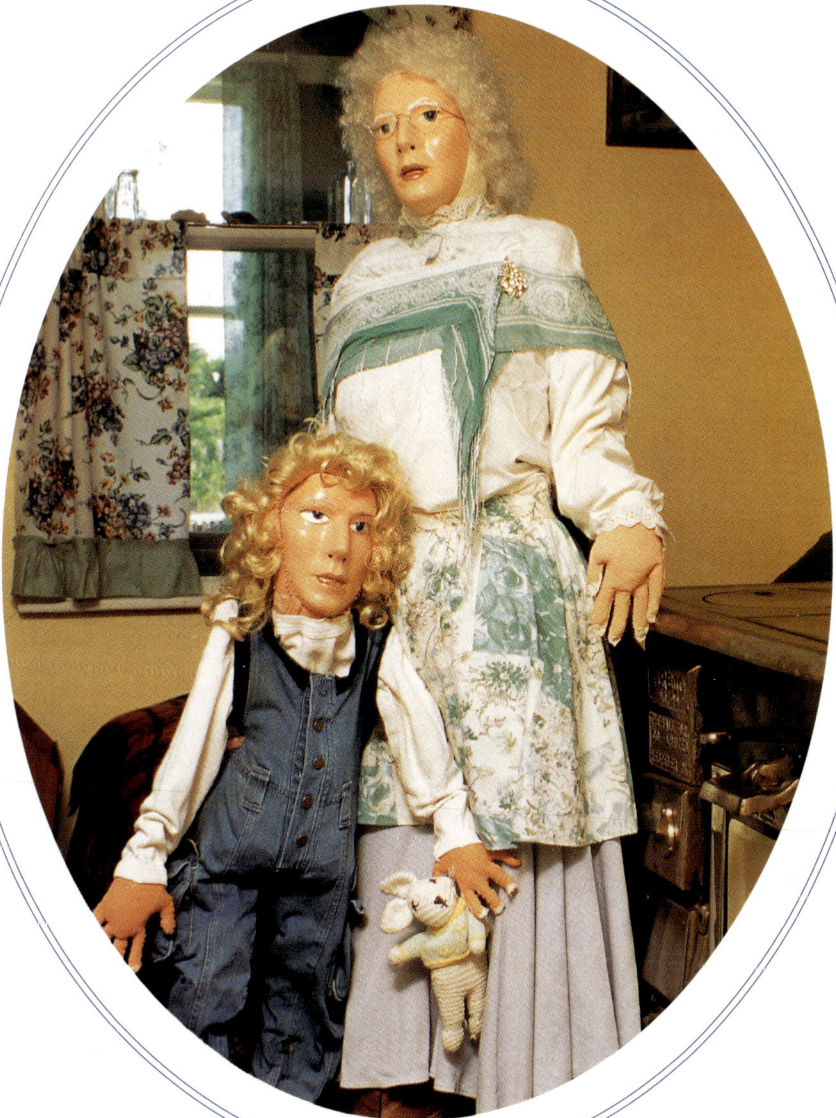

NIMBUS PUBLISHING LTD

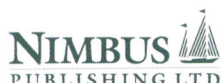

Copyright © Angella Geddes, 1996

All rights reserved. No part of this book covered by the copyrights hereon may be reproduced or used in any form or by any means—graphic, electronic, or mechanical—without the prior written permission of the publisher. Any request for photocopying, recording, taping, or information storage and retrieval systems of any part of this book shall be directed in writing to the Canadian Reprography Collective, 379 Adelaide Street West, Suite M1, Toronto, Ontario, M5V 1S5.

Nimbus Publishing Limited
P.O. Box 9301, Station A
Halifax, Nova Scotia
B3K 5N5
(902) 455-4286

Design: Arthur B. Carter, Halifax
Photos: John Davis, Halifax
Printed and bound in Hong Kong
by Everbest Printing Co. Ltd.

Canadian Cataloguing in Publication Data
Geddes, Angella.
The scarecrows of Necum Teuch
ISBN 1-55109-154-2
I. Title.
PS8563.E33S32 1996   jC813'.54   C95-950291-2
PZ7.G43Sc 1996

For Timothy

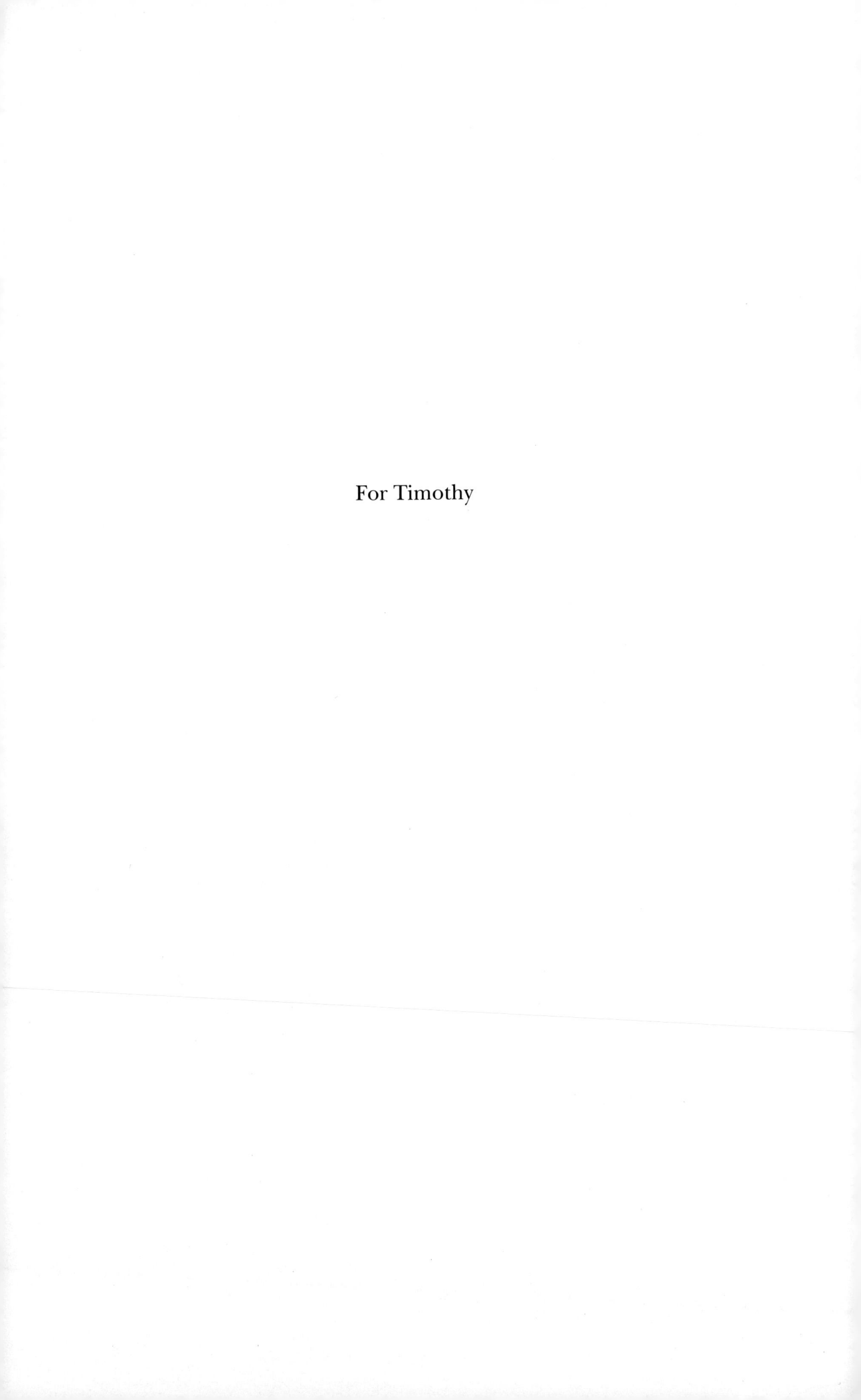

What the Scarecrows are all about

*E*ach year, when a comical looking figure would appear in my dad's vegetable garden, I'd know for certain it was spring. The floppy ill-clad figure by the garden gate came to be a part of summer and a part of home.

In the autumn of 1987, my dad passed away. The following spring brought home afresh the sad loss—no scarecrow would appear from Dad's workshop.

As flowers sprung up and days grew warmer, the garden seemed empty and lonely without a scarecrow at the usual post. I decided to try to make one. Once in place, it did make me

feel better. It evoked happy memories. Kind friends and residents of the Moser River, Necum Teuch, and Ecum Secum areas told me they liked the gesture. They, too, had missed the familiar figures.

My first scarecrow wasn't very good. I resolved to make a better one the next year. I became zealous in my efforts. The ridiculous menagerie on my lawn is the result.

The scarecrows are meant for silly, light-hearted fun—we all need a little of that in our lives.

A scary Legend

*A*long the eastern shore of Nova Scotia, there is a seaside settlement known as Necum Teuch (pronounced Neecom-Taw). In Necum Teuch there is an old white farmhouse nestled in a woodsy dell. On one side of the

house, there is an unruly garden. In this garden, birds sing, butterflies fly, flowers flower, and creeping creatures creep. This is not unusual.

On the other side of the house, there is a small green lawn and a little vegetable garden. It seems that the lawn always needs to be mowed, and the vegetable garden always needs to be weeded. Certainly, this is not unusual.

In front of the house, there is a wide field. Through the field there is a path leading down to the shore. At the shore, seagulls call out sharply and dart about overhead. Slowly, twice each day, the tide comes in and the tide goes out. Sometimes jellyfish lay sprawled over flat rocks. One of the rocks is called "the white wishing chair," and anyone can sit on it to make a wish.

At the back of the house, there is a forest with a dark and mysterious swamp. I once heard a legend about a creature who lives there. Yes, I did, and that story gave me the shivers. But there are lots of legends. It is not unusual to hear one.

There is something unusual, though, about the yard around the old white farmhouse in Necum Teuch. It is filled with scarecrows! Yes, in the gardens, on the lawn, and around the house, there are scarecrows, as still as a hot summer day.

You may wonder how they got there. First, I will tell you the stories behind the scarecrows, for everything has a story. Then I will tell you the legend about the creature that lives in the swamp of the forest. Maybe you will get the shivers, too, just enough to make the story fun.

Aunt Mary

*A*unt Mary is a kind and friendly lady. She smiles and laughs a lot. The local children like to visit her. Together they make raisin cookies and gingerbread men. It is fun to bake things in Aunt Mary's old wood stove.

While they work, Aunt Mary often tells the youngsters stories of when she was a little girl. Things were much different long ago from what they are now. The children like to hear about the old days.

Sometimes Aunt Mary takes the children on picnics. They walk into the woods or across the field and down to the shore. The parents and older folk often go along as well. Many of them remember baking cookies and hearing Aunt Mary's stories when they were children. You see, she is a very old lady. She may be the oldest person in Necum Teuch.

Aunt Mary likes to work in her garden. She says her favourite flowers are the yellow honeysuckle because if you take a big sniff before going to bed, you will dream of something lovely. And what's more, if you wish hard enough, your dream will come true. She has many sayings like that. Visiting her is always fun.

Everyone loves Aunt Mary. But no one loves her more than little Timothy Daniel does. She lets him lick the cookie batter from the bowl.

Captain Smith

Captain Smith is an interesting sort of man. He travels all around the world on a huge ship. When he comes home to Necum Teuch, he brings presents for everyone and new stories to tell.

In the evenings, family and neighbours gather in Aunt Mary's kitchen. They sit around and listen to the captain's adventures at sea. He talks of places and people in faraway lands. When his sea chest is carried home from the wharf landing, everyone likes to look in it to see all of the curious things he has collected.

Sometimes, Captain Smith tells scary ghost stories. But when he sees frightened looks on the children's faces, he always laughs, slaps his knee, and winks. Then he assures them the stories are not true as he passes out peppermints from a bag in his pocket.

Little Timothy Daniel always pretends to be more frightened than he really is so he will get extra peppermints. Captain Smith knows this, but he doesn't mind. He just chuckles and calls him a scamp.

On these special evenings, Aunt Mary and some of her friends make tea and serve a big lunch. Sometimes Jonathan Smythe plays his fiddle. People clap their hands in time to the music. Everyone dances. It is always a happy time when Captain Smith comes home from sea.

Jonathan Smythe

Jonathan Smythe is a big, big fellow. He lives in a log cabin in the green woods of Necum Teuch. He works at the local mill. He is terribly shy, but he likes to guide the children on hikes through the woods. He knows all kinds of wonderful things about the animals and the forest. He can even find chewing gum growing on trees.

Sometimes Jonathan will play his fiddle at a picnic or a party, but he has to be coaxed to do it. He has a knack for making his fiddle sound soft and sort of haunting. It makes people feel something beautiful deep in their hearts.

Jonathan looks as if his thoughts are very far away when he plays like that. Folks often get moist eyes when this happens, and Aunt Mary sniffles a little. Then Jonathan turns very red and begs everyone's pardon. People wipe their eyes, and Jonathan strikes up a lively reel.

It is said that he is the tallest, strongest, and toughest man on the eastern shore. I believe it. You may be surprised to know that Jonathan Smythe also writes books for children. His books are filled with make-believe stories. Don't tell anyone, because it is a secret, but he signs his books "Muriel Lilly." Isn't that a hoot?

It so happens that Jonathan Smythe believes Miss Mary Lou Ingermanson, the local store owner, is the loveliest person he has ever met. He would like to call on her, but he is too shy. If something would just bring them together, a courtship would begin. I'm sure of it.

Miss Mary Lou Ingermanson

Miss Mary Lou Ingermanson owns the general store in Necum Teuch. She also gives piano lessons to interested children. She is a pretty young woman. She always smells of flowers and spice. She lives in a large white house overlooking the river.

She has three cats. Well, she has two cats really, and one bunny who believes he is a cat. His name is Dilly. The cats are Buddy and Levi. They all live at Miss Ingermanson's house. They eat together, play together, and curl up by the stove to nap together. Buddy and Levi purr quite softly. You would laugh if you heard the racket Dilly makes when he thinks he's purring softly too.

Miss Ingermanson is always surprised to read about two cats and a bunny living together in Muriel Lilly's books, which she sells in her store. Some of the adventures described in the books are so similar to the antics of Buddy, Levi, and Dilly that Miss Ingermanson is amazed by the coincidences. She would be even more amazed if she knew that the author of those tales is the man she loves so dearly.

Miss Mary Lou Ingermanson is in love with Jonathan Smythe. She is certain, too, that if he would call on her just once, their courting would begin.

Kelvin Lovely

K elvin Lovely is the student preacher who has lived in Necum Teuch for two years. It is time for him to leave, but he loves Necum Teuch, and he would like to stay. The people here want him to settle in the community. They have asked him to lead the church.

Alas, the young preacher has troubles. He is secretly in love with the school teacher, Miss Marie Marlene. Well, he believes it is a secret. Everyone in Necum Teuch knows about it, except Miss Marlene. She does not know yet that Kelvin has a beautiful diamond ring in a box in his pocket and an even more beautiful dream in his heart.

Kelvin Lovely wants to ask for Miss Marie Marlene's hand in marriage. If she accepts, he will stay in Necum Teuch. If she refuses, he will leave the community and return to his home in Upper Middle Musquodoboit.

Kelvin Lovely is not hopeful that Miss Marlene will accept his proposal. He has his belongings already packed in his trunk, ready for a hasty departure, I bet.

Miss Marie Marlene

Have you ever sat on pins and needles? Neither has Miss Marie Marlene, but she imagines that she knows just how it would feel. That is because she is quite in love with the young student preacher. She does not know for certain if he has the same feelings for her. Waiting and hoping for him to say something is like sitting on pins and needles. Soon he will be leaving the community.

Sometimes, at a dance or a party, Miss Marlene thought she saw a thrilling sparkle in Kelvin's eyes when he looked at her. He often walked her home from Bible study. He visited her very frequently at home, and he was a regular guest at the Marlene family supper table. What could it all mean?

She has another reason to hope his visits mean something. You see, Kelvin Lovely kissed her once in Aunt Mary's flower garden, beside the honeysuckle bush.

Tomorrow, there is going to be a bake sale at the first fair ever held in Necum Teuch. Miss Marlene expects that Kelvin will buy her pie at the sale. Perhaps he will say something then. Just now, she feels so distraught that, if he says nothing at all at the fair, she may lose her nerves. Yes, in sheer frustration, she just may dump her pie over Kelvin Lovely's head!

Her reputation would be ruined though. She'd never again be known as the respectable Miss Marie Marlene. No, she would then be known as the rowdy, rude school teacher who once dumped a pie over the student preacher's head. Oh dear!

Captain von Veiderzaem

Captain von Veiderzaem is the captain of a ship that stops every so often at the wharf in Necum Teuch. Always there is cargo loaded and unloaded onto his ship for communities along the eastern shore.

The captain never fails to visit Aunt Mary on his trips to Necum Teuch. He does not speak English very well. He once told Aunt Mary that her molasses cookies were "unspeakable." He meant that he could not say how delicious they were.

Sometimes, the captain invites everyone to come on board his ship, and there is a party. He sings happy German songs. Lots of people dance and clap along. We have great fun.

Captain von Veiderzaem once gave Aunt Mary a recipe for something called "kartoffel soup." Aunt Mary wasn't sure that he had translated the ingredients into English quite correctly. She made it anyway. Everyone agreed that it was—well—it was "unspeakable!"

Long ago, Pappy Smith sailed from his homeland to Necum Teuch. He was just a lad then.

Now Pappy Smith is a great-great-grandfather. He has children and grandchildren who love him and help take care of him. Pappy Smith loves them in return. In fact, he loves everyone in Necum Teuch. He has an especially soft spot in his heart for Timothy Daniel. He says that Timothy Daniel makes every tomorrow exciting.

Pappy Smith likes to sit on the cellar house step and recall his younger days. He remembers the first time he saw his wife, Mabel. She had stepped into her family's cellar house to put away the milk and butter to keep them cool. He had fallen head over heels in love with her at that moment.

Later, they shared their first kiss in her parents' cellar house doorway.

Now Pappy Smith is often warned to stay away from the cellar. Kind folk are concerned he will fall down the stairs. Recently, Pappy Smith did fall into the cellar house. Fortunately, he wasn't hurt.

"That isn't the first time I fell head over heels in a cellar house," he chuckled. Nobody knew what he meant, but Pappy Smith enjoyed the joke.

Timothy Daniel

There are lots of children in Necum Teuch. Timothy Daniel is one of them. He is four years old. His parents give him a hug each night at bedtime. This is when he is the most cuddly and lovable because he is tired out from playing all day.

In the daytime, Timothy is a whirlwind of activity. Sometimes he dangles upside down from tree branches. Almost every day he chases Miss Ingermanson's cats, Buddy and Levi. He is always into mischief, and he is always doing it with gusto.

Not long ago, Timothy Daniel had laryngitis. It affected him in a strange way. It made his voice sound loud and deep. His mother called Timothy her little foghorn. She told him to stay indoors. But he quickly forgot and out he went. Before his mother could call him back inside, Timothy was running home.

He was very excited. His eyes looked like two big blue saucers.

"I saw a 'hop!'" croaked the little boy with the great big voice. "A hop!" Timothy put a hand beside each of his ears and wiggled two fingers on either side. Then he hopped into the house.

"Oh, you've seen Miss Ingermanson's rabbit, Dilly," laughed Timothy's mother.

"Yes!" boasted Timothy Daniel. "I saw a hop!"

The Stink

*A*unt Mary laughed when she heard about Timothy Daniel and the rabbit. She knit him a white bunny to play with. Timothy calls it his hop, and he takes it with him wherever he goes.

One evening, on the way to church, Timothy Daniel spied wildflowers growing near the church doors. He asked his mother if he could pick some for Aunt Mary.

"Yes, you may," said his mother, "but be quick. Church is about to start, and I don't want you to be late." Timothy was delighted. He liked to surprise people with presents, especially Aunt Mary. He hummed a happy tune as he gathered a bouquet.

What happened next was not his fault. Not really. While Timothy Daniel was picking flowers, a sudden gust of wind came up. That was certainly innocent enough. The wind blew a big brown paper bag within Timothy's reach. He grabbed it and peeked inside. It was empty. There was no harm done there.

But things took an unfortunate turn. Just after the bag appeared, Timothy spotted a small animal a few feet away. It was beautiful, with a shiny black coat and a tidy white stripe down its back. Timothy wanted to show it to his friends in church.

We know that, usually, such an animal could not be coaxed into a paper bag. Neither could it be lugged awkwardly into a church by a four-year-old boy—not without incident. Nevertheless, Timothy caught the animal in the paper bag and carried it inside the church.

He started up the aisle just as the choir began to sing. At that moment, the unexpected guest leaped out of the bag. We all know what skunks do, and this one did it! Oh my!

Timothy yelled with surprise. He hurried about the church, trying to catch the skunk.

"Here stink," he called.

Everyone rushed out of the building. Miss Marie Marlene giggled behind her handkerchief. She had noticed Kelvin Lovely duck behind the pulpit. She assumed that he was horrified. In fact, he was in fits of laughter.

Captain von Veiderzaem pointed at Timothy Daniel and tried to look cross, but he broke into a hearty laugh instead.

The skunk soon wandered outside. Everyone slowly headed home, still talking about the skunk.

Jonathan Smythe had gallantly led a white-faced Miss Mary Lou Ingermanson outside to fresh air. He even offered to walk her home.

The very next day Miss Ingermanson sent Timothy Daniel a big bag of candy. Yes, she did.

Timothy was not punished for the incident, which was more like an accident anyway. The scent of the skunk had made him quite ill. While Timothy lay recovering in bed, he told his mother that he hoped Aunt Mary wouldn't knit him a stink.

*N*ecum Teuch may seem like an idyllic place to live. Everyone gets along, and everyone seems to be well and happy. So they were. But the tale of Necum Teuch has a surprising twist.

According to legend, an ugly, selfish creature lives in the swamp of the forest, behind the old white farmhouse. He is called the Swamp Soggon. He is made of mud through and through, for he has a mean spirit. He does not like anyone to enjoy anything at all. He hates to see children smile. He detests laughter. The people of Necum Teuch were far too happy for the Swamp Soggon. From the swamp, he could hear their laughter and music. It made him feel lonely and bitter.

As the legend goes, when the Swamp Soggon heard the people of Necum Teuch were planning a fair, it was too much! He decided to spoil their happiness by casting a spell from an old witch's Book of Spells.

On the evening before the fair, the Swamp Soggon crept out of the swamp. He cast the spell and ran away, just as happy as a Swamp Soggon could be. He had changed everyone—almost everyone—in Necum Teuch into scarecrows! What a terrible thing to do! As Captain von Veiderzaem might say, "It was unspeakable!"

Will the Scarecrows of Necum Teuch ever become real people again, you may ask. If they do, it will only happen because of Timothy Daniel. You see, Timothy Daniel was perched on the low shed roof at the old white farmhouse when the Swamp Soggon first appeared. Timothy Daniel had been told not to climb on shed roofs, but he had forgotten. He and his hop were being famous mountain climbers.

Just as Timothy reached the roof and stood up tall, he saw something dreadful. It was the Swamp Soggon lurking at the edge of the swamp! Timothy heard the hateful spell that the Swamp Soggon was chanting. Before he could scramble down to run for help, Timothy began to tingle all over. His little arms and legs felt stiff. He knew he was changing into a scarecrow! Time was beginning to stand still.

"Tomorrow will never come now," thought Timothy sadly.

He thought of the fair and the fun he and the other children would miss. He thought of the molasses cookies which Aunt Mary planned to sell in the bake sale. He thought of the taffy pull and the three-legged race. There was supposed to be a big picnic supper and music on Captain von Veiderzaem's ship, too.

The longer Timothy thought about tomorrow, the more excited he became. Soon, he felt very excited indeed!

Suddenly, the tingling stopped. Timothy Daniel found that his arms and legs were no longer stiff at all!

The last time I saw Timothy Daniel, he was in Aunt Mary's flower garden, picking a big bunch of yellow honeysuckle.

What do you suppose will become of those Necum Teuch Scarecrows? Timothy Daniel seemed to know the answer. He hurried off, though, to the white wishing chair before I could ask him. But like Pappy Smith, I have a feeling that Timothy Daniel will make tomorrow very exciting indeed!

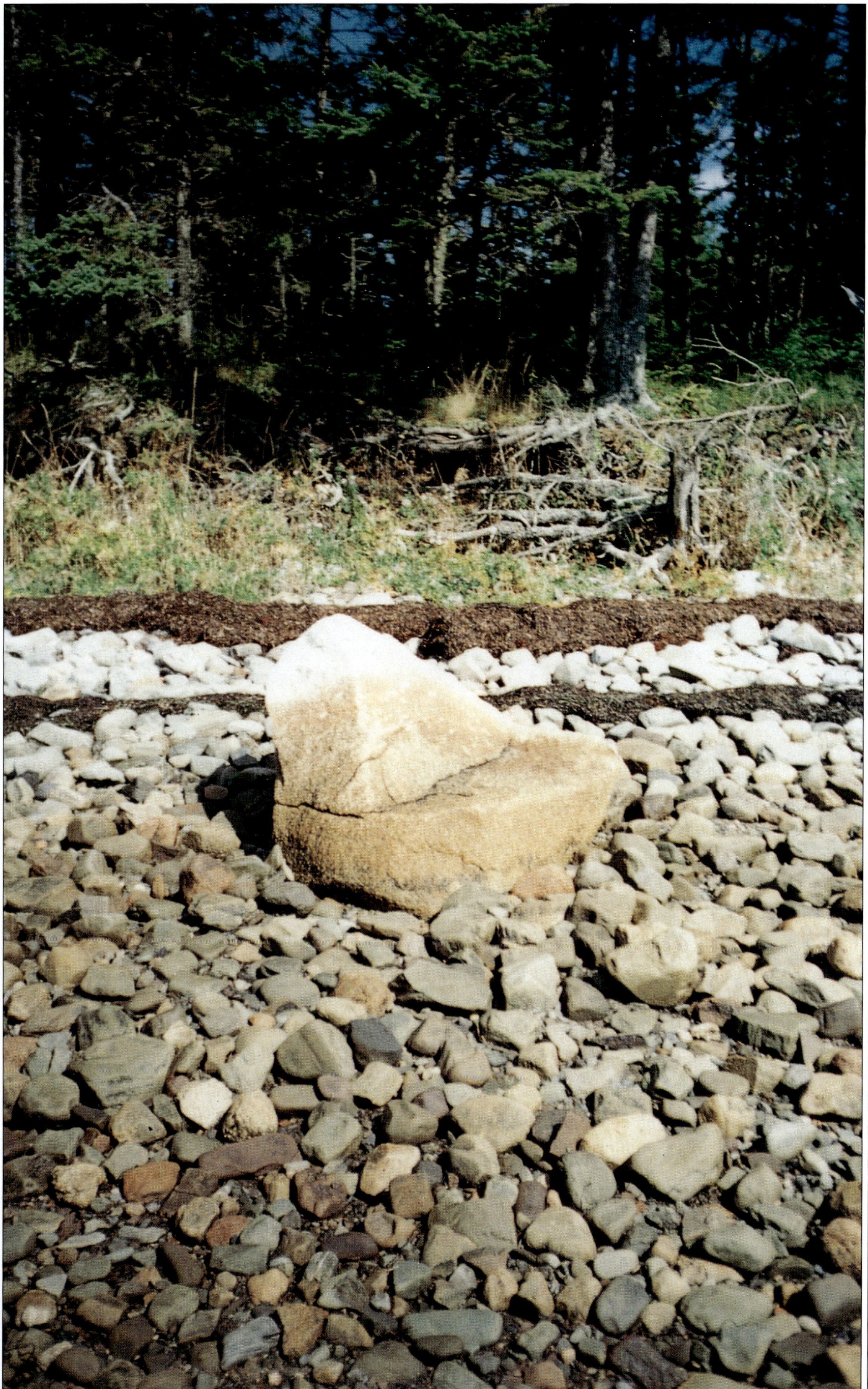

Kartoffel Soup

Here is the recipe for Kartoffel Soup given to Aunt Mary by Captain von Veiderzaem:

    3 generous cups potatoes, cubed

    1 large onion, finely chopped

    ½ cup salt pork, cubed

    ¼ cup butter

    ¼ cup flour

    1 pint (2 cups) blend or milk

    1 cup broad beans or lima beans

Cook potatoes and onion together. Set aside. Fry salt pork cubes until crisp. Set aside. In a large pot, melt butter and add flour. Let mixture brown lightly. Slowly add blend or milk while stirring with whisk. As blend or milk heats, the mixture will thicken. Hot water may be added for desired thickness. Add potatoes and onions, pork, and beans. Heat well.

Top with sour cream. Serve with thick chunks of bread toasted in oven and generously buttered.

Making a Scarecrow

It is quite easy to make your own scarecrow, and there is certainly room for imagination. In fact, the more you use your imagination, the more fun it will be.

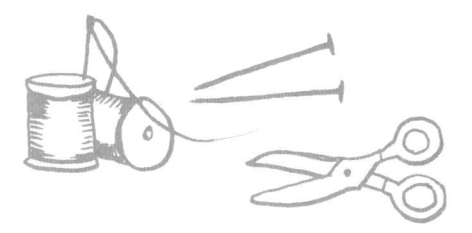

First, please remember to ask an adult to help you when using needles, nails, scissors, or any other sharp tools.

To begin, you will need some old clothes. Your parents, grandparents, neighbours, or friends may have some you could use. There are also many used clothing stores which stock bins especially for costumes. You may find that many stores have masks and wigs on sale, especially after Halloween. You could use a mask, or you could draw a face on your scarecrow. Old dust mops make great hairdos. Hats can add a lot of fun. Mittens or gloves make good hands if they are stuffed. Extra plastic grocery bags and rags make good stuffing.

You could start your scarecrow by stuffing a sweater sleeve to the size and shape of the head you want to make. Tie each open end firmly with string and cut off the extra material. Next, stuff a shirt or sweater and tie the arms at the end. How much stuffing you use will determine how fat or thin, bumpy or smooth, your scarecrow will be. Now you can sew the stuffed mittens or gloves onto the arms. The next thing to do is stuff a pair of slacks, pants, or nylon stockings and tie them at the feet. These will be the legs of your scarecrow.

Now you are ready to put it all together. First, tie or sew the head onto the stuffed shirt or sweater. Your scarecrow will certainly need a head! Next, attach the legs—the stuffed pants or slacks—onto the shirt. A darning needle and strong thread are the best materials to hold these parts together.

Once the head, body, and legs are together, you have a basic scarecrow!

Now, the real fun begins. It is time to dress your scarecrow. If you are drawing a face, be sure to use bright, clear colours. If you are using a mask, you can glue or tie it in place. The same is true for hats and wigs. Old boots and shoes can be used for feet. The costume you have chosen goes on next. It could be a dress for a lady, or a suit for a gentleman. Have you considered a clown or a pirate? Perhaps you will make an Aunt Mary or a Timothy Daniel. Wouldn't that be a hoot?

Remember, the more you use your imagination, the more interesting your scarecrow will be!

If you want your scarecrow to stand, you could tie it to a tree. Or, you could ask an adult to put a post in the ground. An adult will have to help you fix your scarecrow to the post. If you decide to have your scarecrow in a sitting position, you could prop it up in a chair or against a wall or tree.

When you have your scarecrow in place, invite your friends over to see it. Perhaps they will help you pick a name for it. Maybe you will all play a game of Scarecrow.

The Scarecrow Game

The Scarecrow Game is fun to play. You don't need to remember a lot of rules. It's best if you like to be silly and noisy and to play outside. And the wilder and more care-free your imagination is, the better for the game.

First, a clothespin is put into a container for each person playing. One person is chosen to be "it." He or she is then called "Timothy Daniel" and turns away from the rest of the group.

While Timothy Daniel counts to anywhere between five and fifteen, the other players make silly faces and poses. When Timothy Daniel chooses—before he reaches the count of fifteen—he calls out, "Scarecrow," and turns around.

The other players must stay still in their poses without moving at all. Anyone who giggles or moves is "out" for the next round. He or she receives a clothespin. The person who Timothy decides has the funniest pose becomes Timothy for the next round.

When the clothespins are all gone, the game is over. Whoever has the least number of clothespins is the winner of the game.

If you have costumes left over from making scarecrows, you could wear them while playing the game. You could dress up like one of the scarecrows of Necum Teuch!

Scarecrows and Wishes

On a trip in Nova Scotia,

Driving east, guess what I saw?

Some mysterious funny shaped figures,

Called the Scarecrows of Necum Teuch.

There's a rock on the beach near the scarecrows,

It is called the white wishing chair,

For that is its shape and its colour,

And wishes are whispered there.

If you'd like to visit the scarecrows,

And make a wish while you're there,

Then I will share the secret

To finding the wishing chair.

Two things you'll need for the journey,

Without them you cannot leave.

Those things are imagination,

And a heart that can make believe.

Head straight for Musquodoboit,

Pass Petpeswick and Jeddore.

Through Chezzetcook and Clam Harbour,

Go along the eastern shore.

Pass Mushaboom and Quoddy,

Then Harrigan Cove and Moose Head.

Slow down through Moser River,

For the scarecrows are just ahead!

Old Necum Teuch is your port of call,

The Scarecrows will dazzle your eyes,

Then climb up on the wishing chair,

Pretend. Make a wish. Claim your prize.

The Tea Party

Upstairs in my grandmother's attic,

There's a box just full of old clothes,

There are pantaloons, coats, and dresses,

And a floppy old hat with a rose.

There are sweaters, skirts, and aprons,

There are canes and caps of all kinds,

I love to dig in that clothes-box,

For I never know what I might find!

I once put on a long apron,

And a hat with an old lacy veil!

I hobbled downstairs on a wooden cane,

Pretending to be old and so frail.

"Oh, it's my dear old neighbour,"

said Gram, when she spotted me,

"Well, I haven't seen you for ages,

Sit down and I'll make us some tea!"

I tried to make my voice older,

But grandma has such a good ear!

So I spoke through an old lace hanky,

"I haven't been well, my dear!"

Oh, what a job not to giggle,

When grandma looked all around,

"I'd like you to meet my granddaughter,

But it seems that she's not to be found!"

When grandma set out her best china,

I felt so guilty, you see,

That I tore off my hat and cried loudly,

"Oh, look, Grandmother, it's me!"

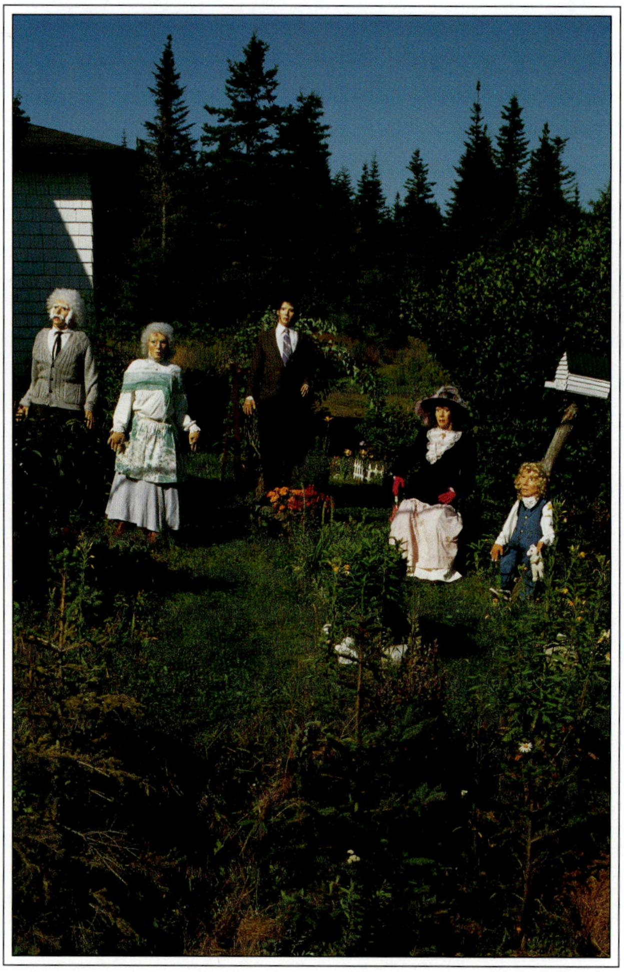